This edition first published in the United States in 2002 by MONDO Publishing, by arrangement with Siphano Picture Books, Ltd., London.

For information, contact:
MONDO Publishing
980 Avenue of the Americas
New York, NY 10018
Please visit our website at www.mondopub.com

Printed in Italy
First Mondo printing October 2001
ISBN (hardcover) 1-58653-855-1
ISBN (paperback) 1-59034-012-4
07 08 09 10 11 12 PB 9 8 7 6 5 4 3 2
01 02 03 04 05 06 07 08 09 HC 9 8 7 6 5 4 3 2 1

Originally published in London in 2000 by Siphano Picture Books, Ltd.
Typesetting and cover design for this edition by Eri Utsunomiya.

Library of Congress Cataloging-in-Publication Data available upon request.

Quentin Gréban

Nestor

MONDO

Little Nestor hated cleaning up in the morning. He always fidgeted while his father was picking the bugs and twigs out of his hair. But this morning he sat quietly and didn't complain, because he had something very important to ask his father.

"Please may I go
fishing by myself?"
asked Nestor.

"Only if you promise to
be careful," said his father.
"Stay away from hedgehogs
because they prickle . . . alligators because
they bite . . . and elephants because they're
big and clumsy and might step on you!"

"I'll stay away from them all!" he promised.

When Nestor reached the river, he was surprised to see how crowded it was. He looked for a spot to sit.

Oops—hedgehogs! They didn't look dangerous, but Nestor remembered to keep away from their prickles.

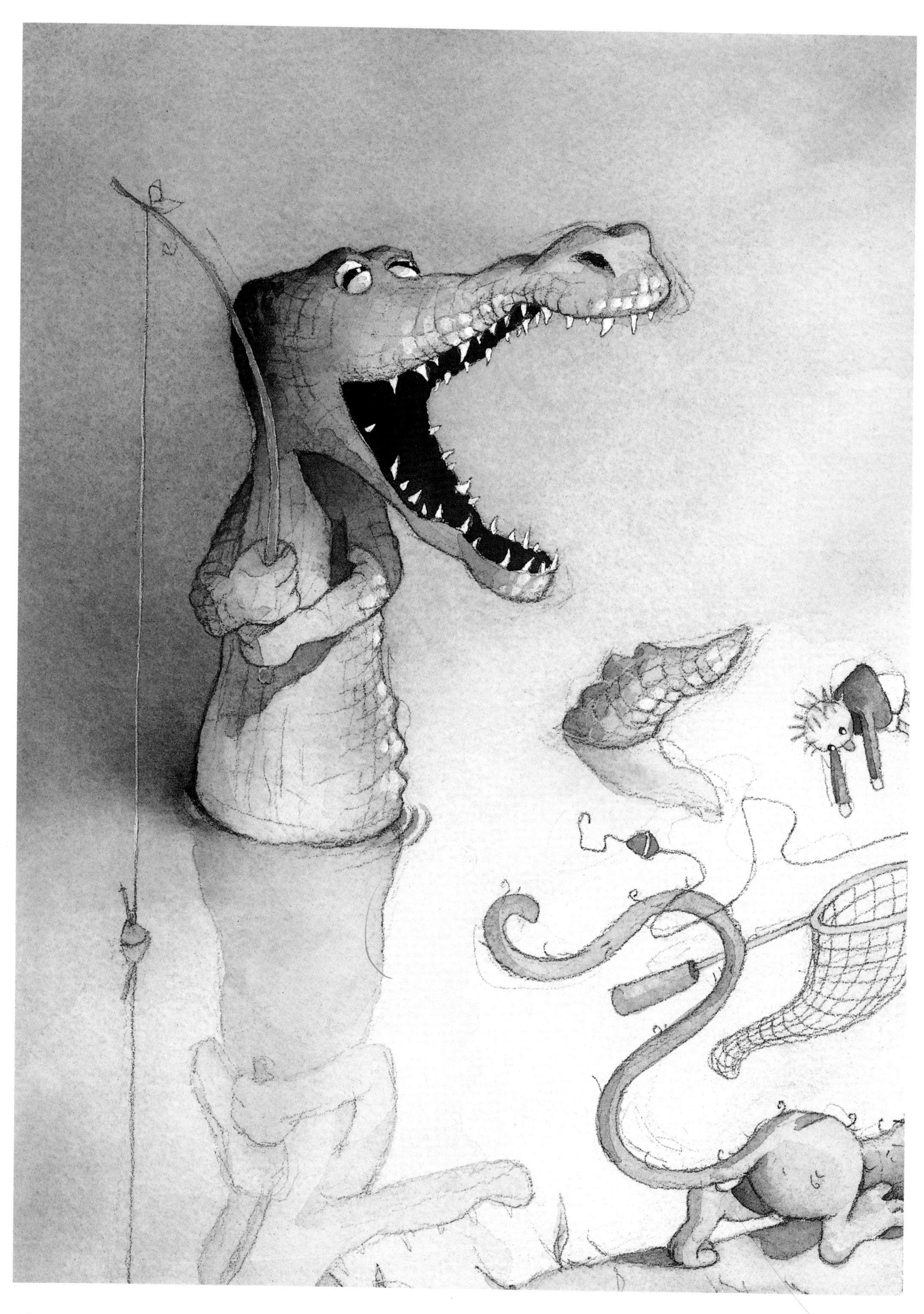

Nestor hurried past an alligator, who greeted him with a big, wide smile.

Further on, he found a comfortable spot all to himself. "Lucky me!" thought Nestor, and cast out his line.

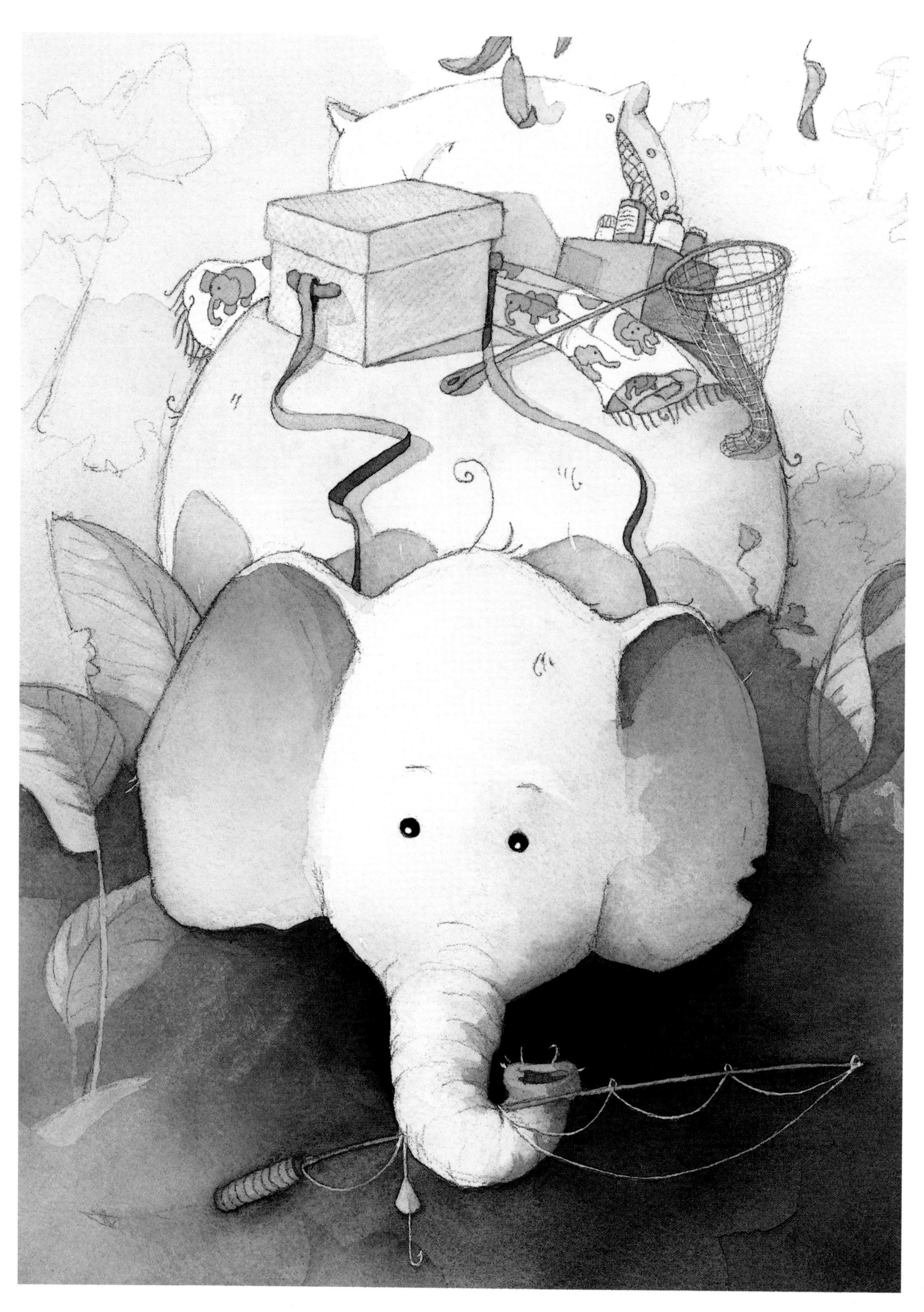

The river was full of fish. Nestor caught one with his first cast. He quickly caught another and another. Nestor was good at this!

Suddenly, Nestor heard a swishing in the bushes. Then he heard a stomp and a crash—and then he saw a huge elephant.

Oh, no! Nestor was supposed to stay away from elephants.

Nestor jumped behind a tree so that he wouldn't get squashed. He watched as the elephant sat down, right on Nestor's spot. "Clumsy elephant!" thought Nestor. "He didn't even see me, and now he's taken my place!"

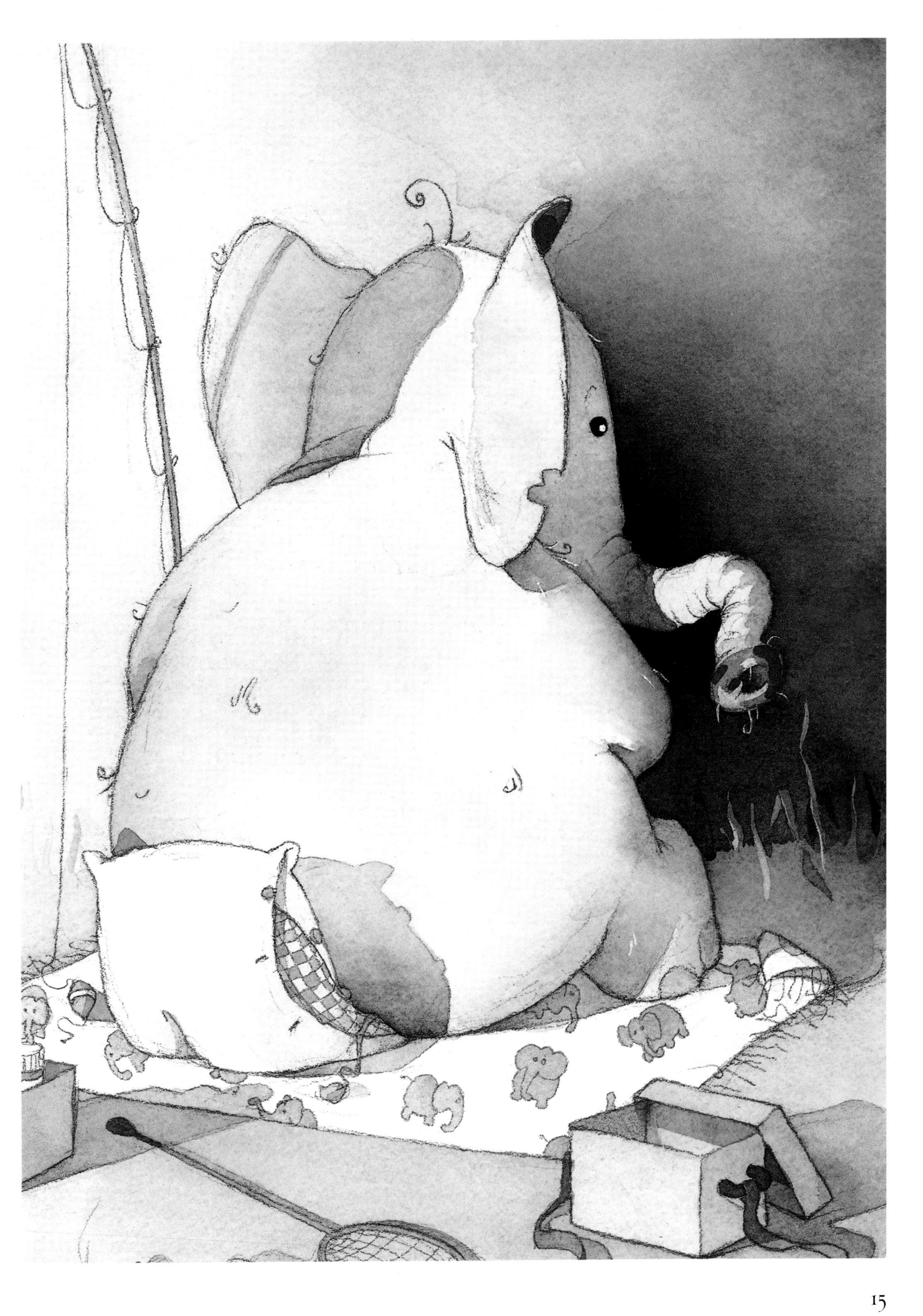

Never mind, he thought.
I'll find another spot to sit.

But all he could find was a branch
hanging out over the river.

Luckily, there were still plenty of fish waiting to be caught. Soon Nestor hooked one. He hung down from the branch, pulling harder and harder. He stretched and stretched . . .

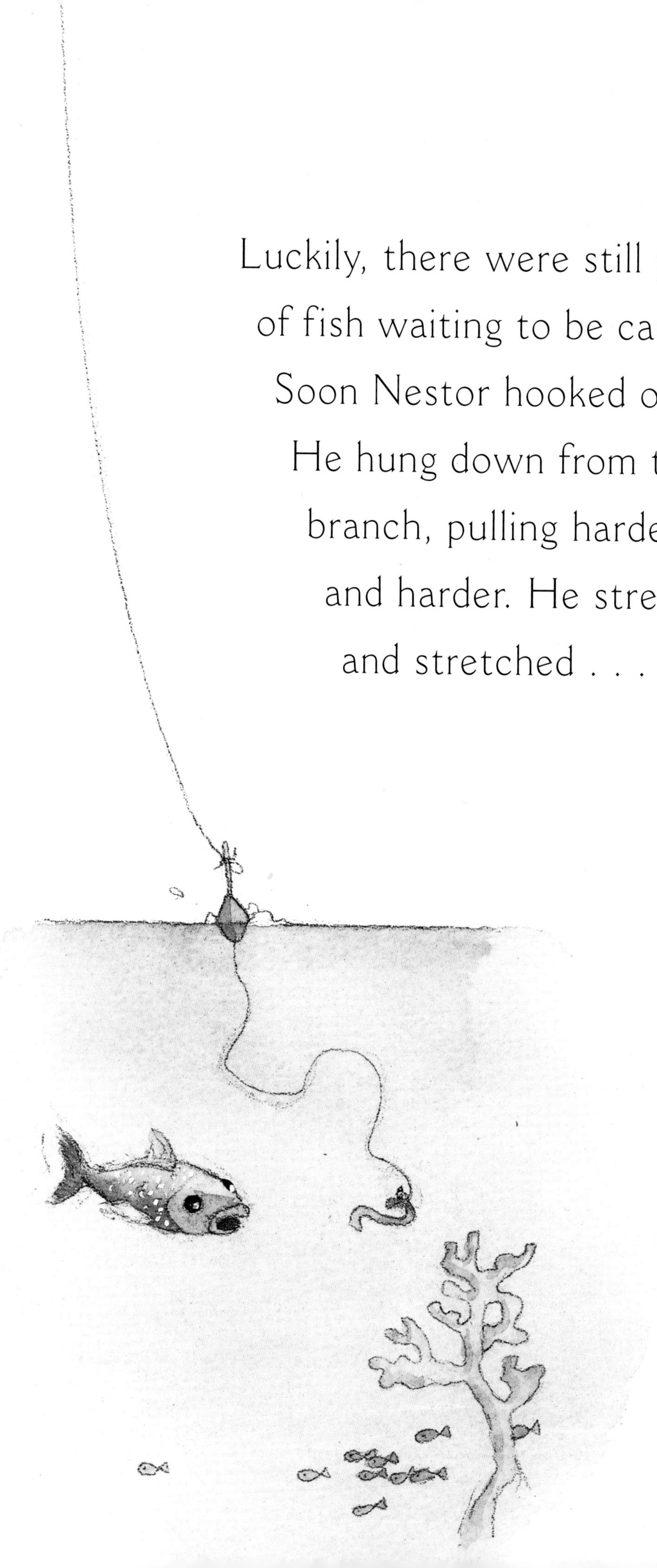

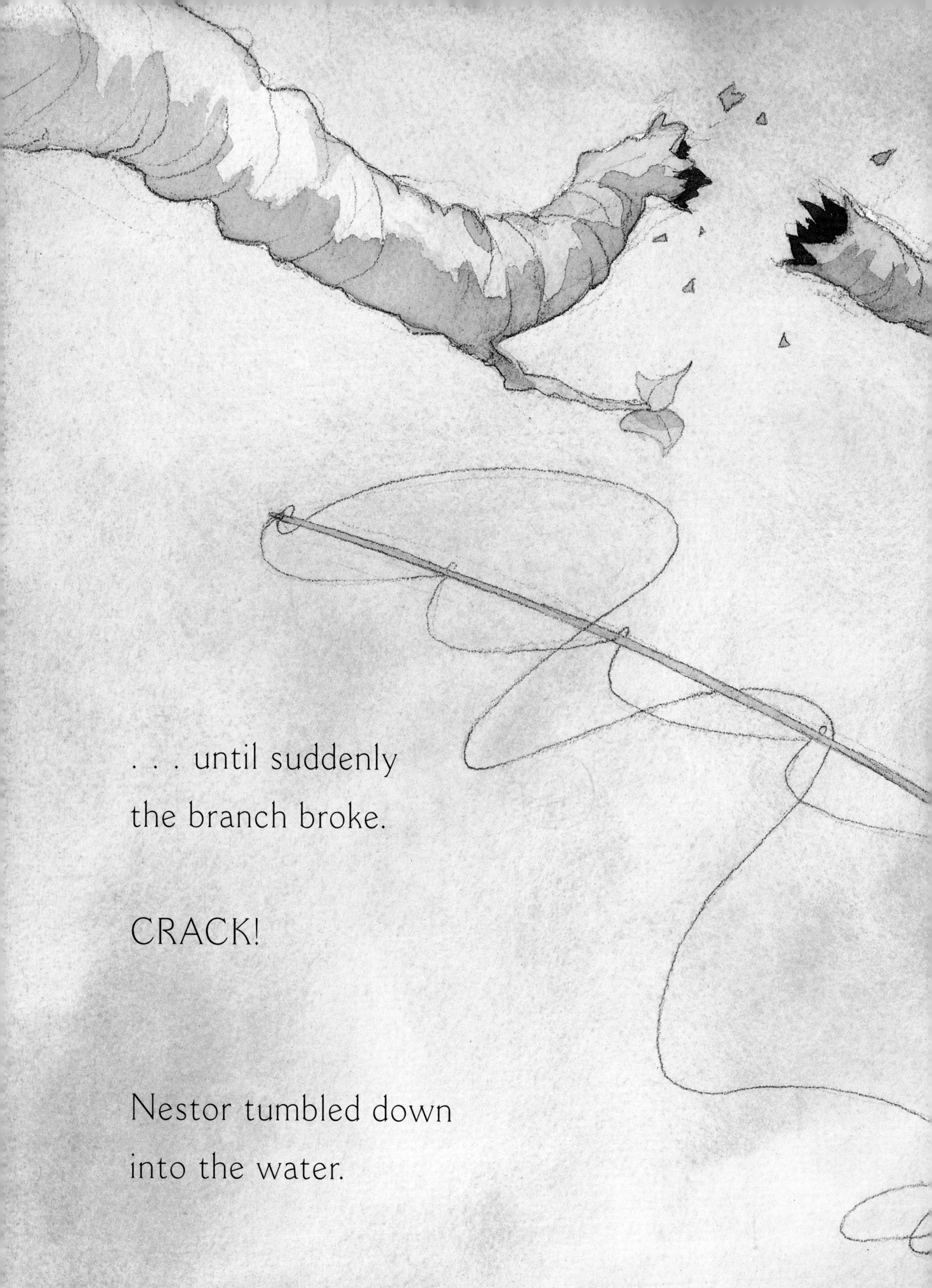

. . . until suddenly
the branch broke.

CRACK!

Nestor tumbled down
into the water.

Nestor tried and
tried to swim to the bank.
If only he could find something to hold on to.

"Help!" cried Nestor. "HELP!"

Suddenly, he saw
something reaching
out to him. It was
the elephant's
trunk!

"Thank you!" cried Nestor, as the elephant swung him up in the air. The elephant waved him about gently to shake off the water. Then he made sure Nestor wasn't hurt and wrapped him in a towel.

What a surprise Nestor's father had that evening. Along with the fish he'd caught, Nestor brought a visitor—and what a big visitor! But Nestor knew the elephant would be careful never to step on him. Now they were friends. They were going to be friends forever!